Saturday because we have people coming for lunch. And not Sunday either because there was something else I can't remember. Anyway it was OBVIOUSLY much more important than my birthday.

She said, poor old Pol, we'll do something nice I promise.

I said, how can it be nice when I will have to spend my birthday at home ITCHING and not being able to see anyone.

When Daddy came home he said, they will put

a big red cross on the door
like they did when people
had Plague.

We did Plague in the
Tudors. It was like very
bad Chicken Pox and lots
of people died of it. The
germs came from rats.
They had fleas only they
were worse fleas than you
get on cats. Rose's cat had
fleas this summer but it
did not have Plague. First

you sneezed then you got

this ring of big spots then

you went black then you

were dead. The Tudors

had lots of Plague. They
went up and down the
streets with carts and
ringing bells and they said,
Bring Out Your Dead and
people put all the dead
bodies on the carts.

I said to Dad, I do not
have Plague and no one is
coming round saying Bring
Out Your Dead.

Dad said, well, not yet,
anyway.

Mopsy started to cry
and said, I don't want to
get the Plague.

I said, you probably
won't unless you meet a
rat with fleas. But you are
going to get the Chicken
Pox because the doctor
said you will and serves
you right.

She cried even more
loudly. It was that silly
crying she does when she

is just showing off but
Mummy got cross and
said, now, Polly, don't be
unpleasant.

Horace my hamster is
not very well either. He is

not eating his hamster
food.

I counted the spots on
my tummy. There are
seventeen. There are spots
on my back too, only I
can't see them to count.
They are on my face too.
I look horrible. I look like
a pizza.

1

Tuesday

Mum let me phone Kelly.
I spoke to Kelly's mum
who is NICE. She said,
oh, poor Polly, you should
have a special treat for
being ill on your birthday.

I said, I agree, but no
one here seems to think it
is anything worth getting
worried about when their
daughter misses the ONLY
ninth birthday she will
EVER have.

Kelly's mum said, oh I
expect they are worried,
poppet.

6

13

20

22

28

29

Grown-ups always stand up for each other, even the nice ones.

Then she said, mind I wouldn't mind missing a few birthdays these days. That is another thing about grown-ups, they always pretend they HATE birthdays but they would not be happy if you forgot to send them a card.

Wednesday

Horace is dead!

He just was dead when Mummy got up this morning.

Thursday

I cried all day yesterday.
Well not quite all day but
nearly.

Daddy said, well I'm
sorry, Pol, but for a
hamster Horace was a
very old man—they only
live about two years and
we'd had him for a lot
more than that.

I said, yes, maybe, but
he was still my hamster
and I am sad that he is
dead.

Dad said, yes, I know
that, and we'll give him a
funeral this evening. Which
was yesterday as I did not
write anything yesterday
because of crying.

This is about Horace dying.

Mummy found him. He
was just dead in his cage.
She said he had died
Peacefully in his sleep.
I saw him.

He is the only dead thing I
have ever seen apart from
flies which don't count. He
looked just like Horace
except he was stiff and
pointy and his fur was
spiky.

Mopsy wanted to see
him. She said, when will
he get better? I said, he is
dead, silly. Dead people
don't get better. She said,
I know but when will he? I
said, he is dead for always
and always. She began to
cry. I said, never mind, he
was a very old man for a
hamster, and she said, no
he wasn't he was a little

hamster boy. She does not understand things. She is only just four.

When Daddy came home we did the funeral. We put Horace in a little box wrapped up in paper handkerchiefs. I put some flowers in the box.

Then Daddy dug a hole at
the end of the garden
under the tree. We all
stood round. Mopsy cried
but I had stopped crying
by then. Dad said,
goodbye, Horace, old
chap. For a hamster you
were really quite nice and
we are going to miss you.

Mummy said, goodbye, Horace, we very much enjoyed having you as one of the family. We will remember lots of things about you.

William came out in his push-chair but he did not say anything except gaa gaa as he is too young.

Mopsy said, goodbye, Horace poo-face. She can be silly like that.

I said, we are very sorry you are dead, Horace. You were very cute and we always liked you except

when you ran away and
when you bit my thumb
that time. I said, I hope
you forgive Mopsy for
that time she tried to
strangle you, she was only

a baby then. Also it was
not kind of her to put you
in the Fisher-Price house
as you did not fit and you
were not a toy as I kept
telling Mopsy only she did
not listen.

Then Daddy said, all
right, Polly, we'll cover
him up now and I'll plant
some daffodil bulbs on top

Then we went in and had green pasta with cheese.

Friday

This is the morning of my absolutely most horrible birthday EVER.

Mummy said, happy birthday, darling, here is your card. I said, it is not going to be a happy birthday as Horace is dead and I have got Chicken Pox.

Mummy said, we will
make it as nice as possible
and don't you want to see
your presents, they are
downstairs?

I said I did.

I went downstairs and
it was a new Arsenal shirt
and these Really Good
trainers! which I need as
my others are getting too
small.

The post came and I
had six cards, one from
Rose who is my nearly-
cousin, one from Kelly,
one from Gran and
Granddad in Scotland,

one from English Granny
and Granddad, one from
Uncle Max in Australia,
and one from Aunt
Sammy and Uncle Phil.

34

Granny phoned and said
could she come over.

She came at three and
said we'd have a proper
old-fashioned birthday
party just like she used to
have when she was a little
girl. Mopsy and me and
Mummy and Granny and
William were there.

Granny had brought fish
paste and cress
sandwiches
(yuck—but she said she
liked them when she
was little), jellies in
paper cases with
bits of peach in
and a cake

she had made with pink
icing on. Granny said
pink icing was really just
the same as white icing
but when she was a little
girl she thought it tasted
better.

For her present she
bought me a Really Nice
backpack in pink and
green. Normally I do not
like pink but this was
Really Nice.

Happy Birthday To *ME*

Brightly

f

Hap-py birth-day to you, Hap-py birth-day to you,

mf

We sang Happy Birthday. I had to join in as there were not enough people there. I sang Happy Birthday to Me. (Mopsy sang Happy Birthday to Me too, even though it was not her birthday.) Then we played old-fashioned games.

G

From good friend

C

G

old friends and new, May good luck go with you, And

We played Oranges and Lemons and Musical Chairs and Pin the Tail on the Donkey. I liked Pin the Tail on the Donkey but Oranges and Lemons was a bit boring. Especially as there were only four of us and Mopsy kept getting things wrong.

Oranges and Lemons

On the whole I prefer
new-fashioned parties but
it was quite fun.

Then the doorbell went
and it was Kelly. She
could not come in because
of the Quorinteen but she
came to the door. She had
a present for me. She had

this HUGE card. Mrs. Shah had written Happy Birthday Polly and we are sorry about the Chicken Pox. She did not know about Horace or I expect she would have written that she was sorry about Horace too. Everybody in the class had signed it.

Josh had signed it!
Everyone says Josh is my
boyfriend BUT HE IS
NOT !!!!! I do NOT have a
boyfriend. Josh is quite
nice though, for a boy.

Kate
x

Josh

HAPPY BIrthday
spotty DARREN
Polly
BIGGS

love Rose
xx

Love from
Alex

HAPPY
Birthday

Darren Biggs had
signed Happy Birthday
Spotty Polly. I hope he
gets Chicken Pox too.

I opened Kelly's
present. It was bubble
bath and strawberry
soap. Mopsy said, she

4   5   6

thinks you need a bath,
hee hee. It was not very
funny. I ignored her.

Wednesday

11

Mopsy was all hot and bad
tempered. Mummy thinks
she has Chicken Pox.

    But I can go back to
school Tomorrow!!!!!

18

Friday

Mopsy is making FAR
more fuss about her
Chicken Pox than I did.
Also she has more spots!

    We have booked my
new birthday party for
three weeks away. I am

going to send out the
invitations today.

Kelly has Chicken Pox
too. It is all Alex's fault.

Saturday

(Not the next Saturday
because I could not be
bothered to write for a bit.
Kelly is back at school
now and Mopsy is back at
nursery. I think that's all
the important things that
have happened up till now.
But the next thing is
REALLY important.)

Mummy and Daddy
said, we have been
thinking. They said,

47

perhaps now Horace is
dead we ought to have
another pet. Though we
know there can never be
another Horace.

I said, goody can we
have a puppy?

BOW WOW

Rubber Puppy

Daddy said, no, we
thought about a dog,
but it would not be fair.
We are out all day and
Mummy will be out all
day when she goes back
to work. We will not be
able to look after a dog
properly.

T for TIGER

Dogs need lots and lots of walks so they can do their poos.

I said, what pet will we have then?

Mopsy said, I want a panda I want a baby tiger I want a koala. She can be quite silly at times. I said, shut up, Mopsy they aren't pets. I said, then can we have a kitten?

Mummy said, that is
what we thought.

I went, WHAT, REALLY ????
They went, yes, really.
I went HOORAY
HOORAY we're going to
have a kitten.

I said, can we get it
from Animal Rescue?

Mummy said, oh you
and your Animal Rescue,
Polly.

I said, well it's nice to
rescue things. Which is
true.

They said, well there is
an Animal Shelter near
somewhere, I forget where,
but not far away.

They gave me the talk
about how kittens would
grow up and become cats

and we would have to look
after it all that time and
how they were NOT TOYS
and did not like being
picked up all the time and
dressed up.

I know all this already so
it was really more for
Mopsy than me. Alex used
to dress their cat up and

now it runs away all the time when it sees her.

I said, can I phone Kelly? She cannot have a cat because they give her mum the heebie-jeebies. The heebie-jeebies are what I get when I see brocerly. They said, yes you can, then I thought maybe it wouldn't be nice to phone her to say, we are getting a cat, when she can't have one. I shall tell her on Monday and she can come and visit our cat when we have one.

Daddy said, that is very thoughtful, Polly.

Well I am more thoughtful than some people.

Saturday

We are going to the Animal Shelter tomorrow!!!!!

Today we went to the pet shop. We bought some cat litter and a cat tray

(yuck), a basket to bring
him back from the shelter in,

a bowl
and some kitten food.

Also some toys—

a ball on a string
and a mouse.

I said to Mopsy,
remember these are cat
toys not toys for you, and
she said, I'm not stupid,
der-brain. Mopsy is
getting quite bossy these
days. Of course, she
wanted to get this little
collar with diamonds on.

It was gross. Mummy
said he won't need a

collar yet anyway. And I said, when he does it will NOT have diamonds on whatever Mopsy says.

I wonder what he will be like. I want a fluffy one but Mummy said fluffy ones are a bad idea as they sick up furballs.

It might be tabby or it might be black and white. I do NOT want a ginger one.

Tomorrow we will have a Kitten !!!!!!!!!!!!!!!

kitte

The Toozleum Cat.

Sunday at ten o'clock

We are going to see the lady at the shelter at eleven. She is called Paula. Mummy says she sounds nice on the phone.

I can't write any more now but I will try and put it all in later if I am not too excited!

Later

I am too excited.

More Later

I am still excited but I am not too excited and they are asleep now so I can write about them.

When we got to the shelter Paula was there. She was nice. She said, come this way, and we went into a room with all these cages. There were lots and lots of cats. Some were ugly and some were

old. Mummy said we were sorry for the old and ugly ones but what we really wanted was a kitten. Paula said she understood.

There were two lots of
kittens. One lot were
blotchy and they looked
cross. I hoped we would
not end up with them.
Then Paula took us to this
other cage and there were
two REALLY CUTE kittens.
One was all black and one
had white blotches on its
face. It was blotchy but

not ugly so I did not mind.
Paula said they had two
brothers who had just
found homes. Their mother
was in the next cage. She
did not seem very
interested in them so I
suppose she was not a very
good mother.

We opened the cage and
Paula let us pick them up
and take them out. They
were much much bigger
than Horace. (I have not
forgotten about Horace. I
will never forget Horace.)
They had little whiskers
and big eyes.

I said, I don't know

which one I like best.
Mopsy said she liked the
blotchy one but she wasn't
sure because she liked the
other. They meowed and
meowed at us. They
Deffinitly wanted to have
us for owners. Paula said,
look they really like you.

Then I said, Mummy
can't we have two of them?
And she said, well . . . in
her changing her mind
voice. I said, go on. She
said, well, I ought to phone
Daddy and see. She had
her mobile so she phoned
Daddy. Then she said, he
says all right we can!!!!

Mopsy said, Hooray
and I said, Hooray and
Paula said, hush, you'll
frighten all the cats.

Then we went to the
desk and there was
another lady there. She
was not nice like Paula,
she was very strict. She
asked us all these

questions about did we
have a garden and would
we take them to the vet.

Then she looked at me
and Mopsy and said, you
do realize that cats aren't
toys, and they won't be
kittens forever and we'll
have to look after them,
and we mustn't keep
picking them up.

I said I knew all that because Alex keeps picking her cat up all the time and now it runs away from her. I said I would make sure that Mopsy didn't keep picking them up and

when William was bigger
I'd make sure he didn't
either. She said, oh dear,
how many children have
you got (to Mummy), and
afterwards Mummy said
she was afraid that she
wasn't going to let us have
the kittens after all.

Anyway in the end she
let us have them. Which
was *Very kind of her I
don't think* as I said
to Mummy in the car because
if we had not rescued them
they would have ended up
on a rubbish dump or
something, so we were
being nice. And from the
way she went on you
would think we were just
being REALLY HORRID.
We said mine was the
black one and Mopsy's was
the blotchy one.
In the car they meowed all
the way home. They have
such little tiny meows. When

we got home we opened
the box and Mopsy's one
went straight behind the
sofa. My one ran around
the room sniffing. I think
my one is much cuter.

We tried to play with
my one but she was too
busy sniffing. She does
not meow, she makes
these funny little squeaks.
Mopsy's one was still
hiding. Then we put some
food out on a piece of
paper on the floor and
Mopsy tried to push food
into my one's mouth.

I told her off but she would
not listen until Mum told
her off too. Her kitten
was still hiding.

M

He did come out in the
end.

I forgot to say my one
is a girl and Mopsy's one
is a boy.

I also forgot to say
what their names are but

1

I can't anyway as we haven't decided yet. At the moment we just call them Squeak and Splotch.

Then we thought Splotch was trying to go to the toilet on the carpet so we had to show him his tray.

I think that's all I'm going to say for now.

Monday

I did not want to go to school because I wanted to look after the kittens. But Mum said I had to— poo!

Splotch has come out from the sofa now. But

13

20

27

28

29

he is a bit of a scaredy-cat, ha ha.

Mum said, what about Salt and Pepper?

We said, No.

She said, what about Marks and Spencer?

We said No NO.

She said, what about Mickey and Minnie?

I said, this is getting silly.

She said, well I'm trying my best.

I said, you can't just say "something and something" and pretend it's a name.

She said, I give up.

Mopsy said, I want to call my one Melanie Jones.

Melanie Jones is her best friend from school. I said, you can't:

a because you can't call a cat somebody Jones and

b because Melanie is a girl's name and your one is a boy.

I was so excited about the kittens that I forgot to put another REALLY important thing.

I AM GOING TO HAVE MY BIRTHDAY
ON SATURDAY.

HAPPY
BIRTHDAY

I said, promise me I
REALLY REALLY am
going to have my
birthday.

Mopsy said, you might not. You might get Bionic Plague.

She means Bubonic. She thought she was being funny and nearly fell over going ha ha ha.

I said, it is all very well to laugh but YOU didn't miss your birthday because of Chicken Pox.

We are not going to McDonald's again. It is going to be much more fun! We are going to this place where you can do ice-skating and then we are going to have Chinese food! It will be really good.

I have asked the same people again. Everyone can come except Kate M which is all right as I am not **partickerly** keen on her.

Alex said, Josh is coming because he is your boyfriend. You love him.

I said, he is not my boyfriend and I do not love him.

She said, yes and you are going to marry him.

I said, I am NOT going to marry him. I do not have to decide now who I am going to marry.

She went on and on and on.

80

Josh is quite nice. I acksherly like him. But he is NoT NoT NoT my boyfriend.

We still do not have names for the kittens.

Squeak—my one—is very clever. She has found out how to go upstairs. She climbs up and then she walks around looking everywhere and going Mwa mwa in this funny

tiny little squeaky voice. I must
give her proper meowing
lessons.

She does not like playing
with her cat toys but there is
this bit of string she really
loves. And she pretends the rug
is a mouse and tries to kill it.

She is really cute. I wish she had a name.

Tuesday

Mum said, it's a pity they aren't both boys because then they could be Wallace and Gromit.

Dad said, what about Wallace and Grometa?

This was not one of his best ideas.

Wednesday

Gran sent a list of names:

Sooty and Sweep (no)

Popeye and Olive Oyl (no)

Marks and Spencer (no for Mummy and still no)

Peas and Carrots (no to Peas)

Plus and Minus (Why?)

Romeo and Juliet (*Deffinitly* no)

Jack and Jill (*boRING*)

Topsy and Turvy

I think she should stop.

Thursday

Mrs. Shah said, shall we all think of names for Polly's kittens?

Kelly said Little and Large.

Alex said Dinky and Winky. This just shows you the kind of person she is. I will NOT have cats called Dinky and Winky.

Jason said Dracula and Vampire.

Darren Biggs said Snot and Booger. He would.

Kate M said Fluffy and Furry.

Karen said Brandy and Whiskey.

SPENCER 1

2

Freddy Billings said
Marks and Spencer.

There were more but I
cannot remember them.
Some of them were quite
silly.

9

MARKS 7

Josh said, why did we
have to have new names.
He said he thought
Splotch and Squeak were
quite good names.

Acksherly, I think he
is right.

He can be quite
sensible for a boy,
sometimes.

21

Friday
Today when Squeak was
washing herself I said

28

29

Squeak to her and she
stopped her washing and
looked up at me. So now
I think it is her name.

Mopsy said Melanie
Jones was not her best
friend today, her best
friend was Jade. She does
not know what a best
friend is if she thinks you
have a new one every day.
So I said, we are not
calling the cat Jade, stupid,
and she said, I didn't say
we were, stupid, and
Mummy said, now now
girls and are we decided on
Squeak and Splotch
because they are quite nice
names after all.

It is my party tomorrow!

We are going in three
cars!!

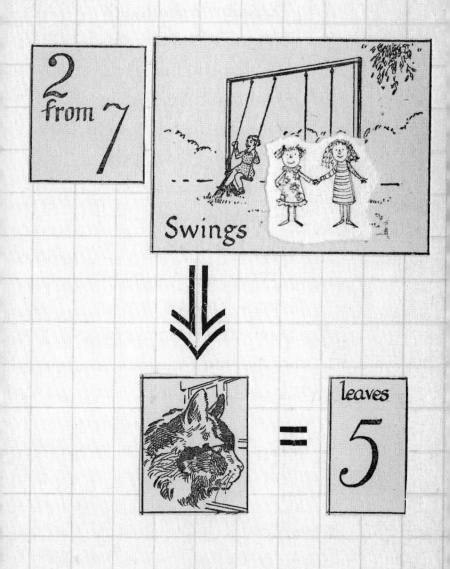

2 from 7

Swings

leaves 5

=

Granny is coming to
look after William, then
Mummy will take me and
Kelly (good) and Alex
(poo) and Josh (good) in
her car and Daddy will
take Mopsy and Kate
and Freddy. Aunt Sammy
will come along with Rose
because they are the same
family. First we are
going to the sports center
for skating then we

快樂

are off to the Golden
Dragon.

歲歲平安添福壽

I will have lots of prawn
toasts and Peking Duck.

Sunday
I am so tired today. It was
really good yesterday.

It was so funny, Alex
goes on and on about how
she always does skating
and how brilliant she is.
Then she fell down
THREE TIMES.

It was so funny. I only
fell down once if you don't
count when Kate bumped
into me and I don't
because that was her fault.

Kelly did not fall down
at all. She is really good.

The boys went all silly
OF COURSE. Sometimes I
wonder what boys are for.
Mopsy is a rubbish skater.
Rose had never done it
before so she did fall down
a bit but she was REALLY
good for a first time.

It was so stupid,
everyone went, Josh is
your boyfriend, and I
went, no he is NOT.

The Chinese food was really nice.

I got good presents. Kelly gave me a video,

Alex gave me a headband with flowers on,

Kate gave me a quite nice pencil case,

Josh gave me a book,

Freddy gave me a box of
fudge

and Rose gave me a
really nice T-shirt.

I said to Josh, it is so
stupid, everyone says you
are my boyfriend, but I
do not have a boyfriend.
He said it is really stupid.
He said his brother has a
girlfriend and all they do
is keep trying to snog.
I said YUCK I was not
going to snog him and
he said he was not
going to snog me.

It was quite late when we got home. I was really tired. Dad said, well, Polly, how do you feel about your birthday now?

I said my birthday was still REALLY HORRIBLE and they were not going to make me forget it EVER. You could not forget Horace dying and being itchy with the Chicken Pox and having to cancel McDonald's.

He said, I know all that, Polly, but did you enjoy yourself today?

I said, oh yes, it was really, really great.

HaPPY BiRthdAY!